To: Michael and Nicholas

10 . 25 . 26

Jerry Pinkney

Enjoy!

The Man Who Kept His Heart in a Bucket

by SONIA LEVITIN

pictures by JERRY PINKNEY

Dial Books for Young Readers 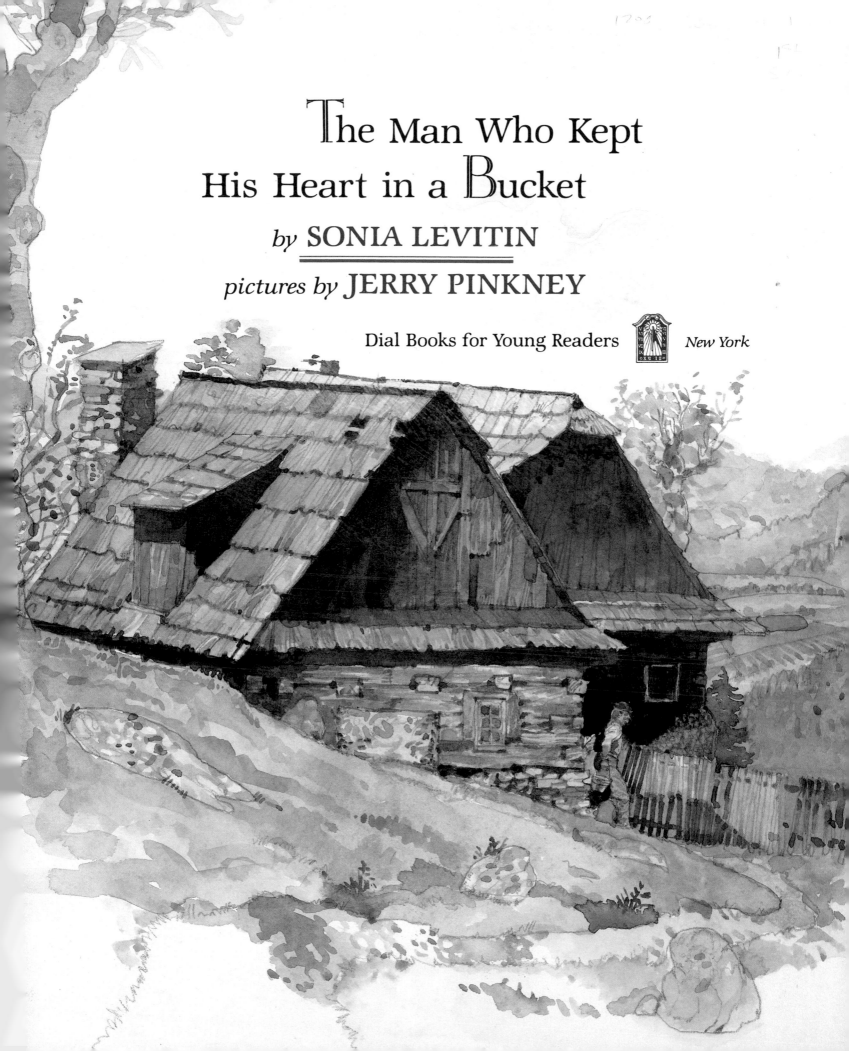 *New York*

Published by Dial Books for Young Readers
A Division of Penguin Books USA Inc.
375 Hudson Street
New York, New York 10014

Designed by Jane Byers Bierhorst
Printed in the U.S.A.
First Edition
1 3 5 7 9 10 8 6 4 2

Library of Congress Cataloging in Publication Data

Levitin, Sonia, 1934–
The man who kept his heart in a bucket
by Sonia Levitin/pictures by Jerry Pinkney.
p. cm.
Summary/Having once had his heart broken,
Jack keeps it in a bucket safe from harm until
one day a young maiden asks him to solve a riddle
which teaches him the true meaning of love.
ISBN 0-8037-1029-1   ISBN 0-8037-1030-5 (lib. bdg.)
[1. Love—Fiction.] I. Pinkney, Jerry, ill. II. Title.
PZ7.L58Man 1991 [E]—dc20 90-20813 CIP AC

The full-color artwork was prepared using pencil, colored pencils,
and watercolor. It was then color-separated and reproduced
as red, blue, yellow, and black halftones.

In a little village far away lived a man named Jack, who kept his heart in a bucket. Jack's heart had once been broken. Now he kept it safe.

Jack worked with metals—gold, copper, and tin. He set out each day to find work, taking his heart along, of course.

His first stop was the baker's.

"You can make me some new pans," said the baker. "And here is a piece of my blackberry pie."

Jack ate the pie, with berries sweet and warm and firm.

"What do you feel when you eat my pie?" asked the baker.

"Full," said Jack. "And thank you kindly."

"Full?" cried the baker. "You don't feel you're in heaven with smell and taste so deliciously sweet?"

"I feel full," said Jack, "and I must be on my way."

By and by Jack came to a piper with a monkey, playing music that set children dancing all along the street.

"You can make me a new tin cup for my monkey to carry," said the piper. "In it we will collect coins for our keep."

"Very well," said Jack, and the piper played a mazurka, so merry that old men tapped their feet, ladies whirled in their skirts, and the children laughed with glee.

"Don't you hear my music?" the piper asked Jack. "Doesn't it make you want to dance?"

"I hear your music," Jack replied, "for it is very loud. But I have no time for dancing. Good day."

On Jack went, till he came to a farmhouse where a poor young couple worked in the field. A tiny baby slept in a sling around the mother's back, making soft sounds like a kitten.

"You can make us a swinging seat for our baby," said the father, "so he can watch us while we work."

The mother said, "We have no money to pay you, but we'll give you garden carrots and potatoes and let you hold the baby in your arms."

"I will take your carrots and potatoes," said Jack, "but let the baby be. I cannot hold little things that squirm and cry."

By and by Jack came to the lake. I need fresh water for my heart, thought Jack. He bent to fill his bucket.

Alas! As he dipped in the bucket, a large golden carp leapt out from the pool, its scales gleaming in the sun.

That fish wants my heart! Jack thought.

Quickly Jack reached into the bucket to save his heart. But in that moment, lo, the carp turned into a beautiful maiden.

And as Jack gazed at the maiden in wonder, she seized the heart and, laughing, danced away with it.

"What a silly man you are," she called, "keeping your heart in a bucket!"

"Give that heart back to me," cried Jack.

"You must catch me first," teased the maiden.

"Thief," cried Jack. "Come back!"

"Don't you know how to play?" called the maiden. "I will tell you a riddle. When you solve it, I shall give your heart back to you."

"Very well," Jack said.

The maiden clambered up into a tree and told the riddle:

"If you would have this heart to hold,
    Find three different scales of gold.
    When you know the three-fold treasure,
    You'll have love in perfect measure."

With that, the maiden ran away, holding Jack's heart in her hands.

Jack went home. That night he could not sleep. He worried and wept, fearing his heart was lost forever.

The next morning Jack rose early and worked. He made pans for the baker, a tin cup for the piper, and a swing for the poor farmer's baby. Then into the furnace Jack threw the bucket that he had kept his heart in. The smoldering red hot fire burned the base metals away, and the pure metal remained, a small round lump. When Jack reached in with his tongs and drew it out, he beheld a small, perfect golden heart.

Jack put the little golden heart into his pocket. He set out on the road until he came to the baker and gave him the new pans.

"Where is your heart?" asked the baker. "I see you did not bring your bucket along."

"A beautiful maiden stole it," said Jack. "I must solve a riddle to win it back."

"Poor Jack," said the baker. "Have a piece of my blackberry pie."

Jack ate the pie, and its sweet, plump lightness thrilled him. "How wonderfully, perfectly delectable and delicious!" he said.

"Thank you," said the baker. "Perhaps your heart is in the right place after all." The baker measured out a small loaf on his scale. Its metal gleamed like gold in the morning sun.

"A golden scale!" cried Jack, clapping his hands with joy.

"I have solved a piece of the riddle. Baker, you must come with me, for perhaps we will need your bread." The baker packed up a loaf of bread, then he and Jack went on. Soon they came to the piper, and Jack gave him the new cup for his monkey.

"Where is your heart?" asked the piper. "You do not have your bucket today."

"My heart has been stolen," said Jack, "but I'm off to get it back."

"First," said the piper, "take time for a little pleasure. I will play for you." The piper played a jig. Jack's feet tickled and tapped. Jack and the baker danced arm in arm.

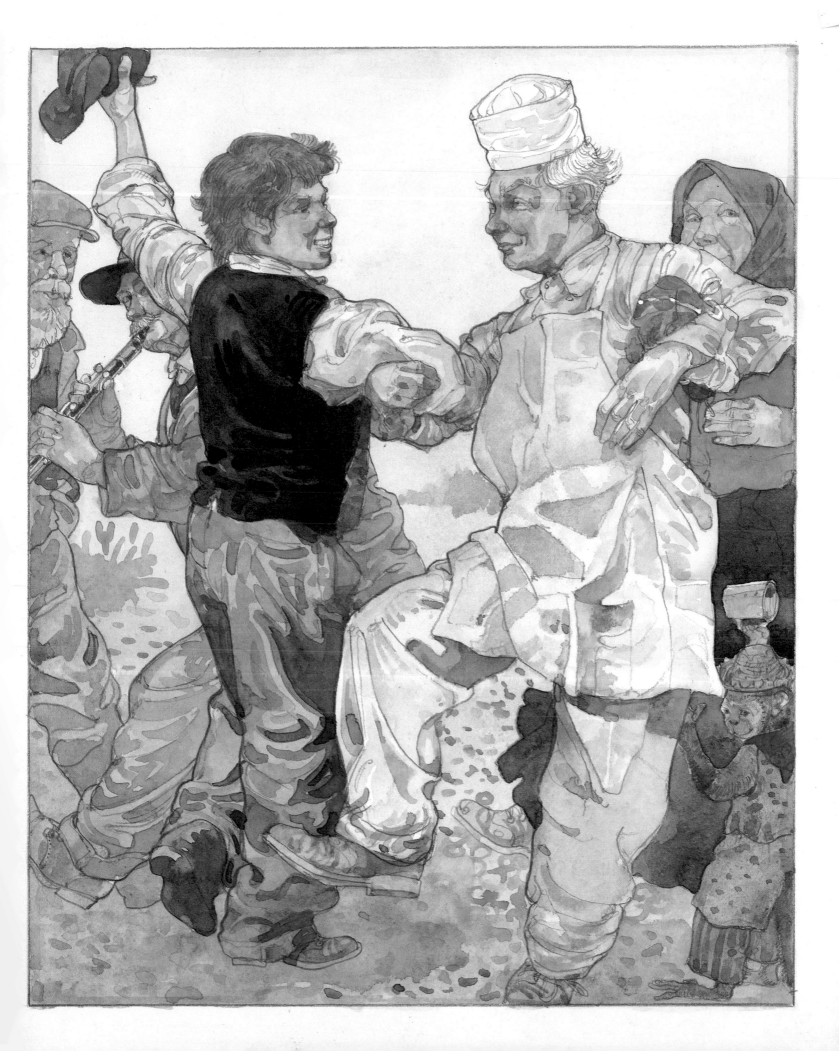

"What wonderful music!" said Jack.

"Thank you," said the piper. "Your heart is in the right place now."
The piper played a set of jumping, running notes, up and down
the scale.

"A golden musical scale," cried Jack. "I have solved the second part
of the riddle. Piper, you must come with us, for we might need
your music."

Jack and the baker and the piper went on until they came to the farmhouse, and Jack gave the mother the new swing for her baby.

"Where is your heart?" asked the mother. "You did not bring your bucket today."

"My heart is not far away," said Jack. "I know because I feel better than ever before."

The mother put the baby into the swing. The baby laughed and clapped his hands with glee. Jack laughed too, and held out his arms. "What a sweet little baby," he said. "I would like to have one of my own."

The mother smiled and said, "Your heart is surely in the right place now."

The baby's father came by with a large golden fish in his net.

Jack saw the bright scales of the fish gleaming in the sun. "There are golden scales on the body of the fish!" Jack said. "Now I know the third piece of the riddle. You must come with me for I need you all, dear friends."

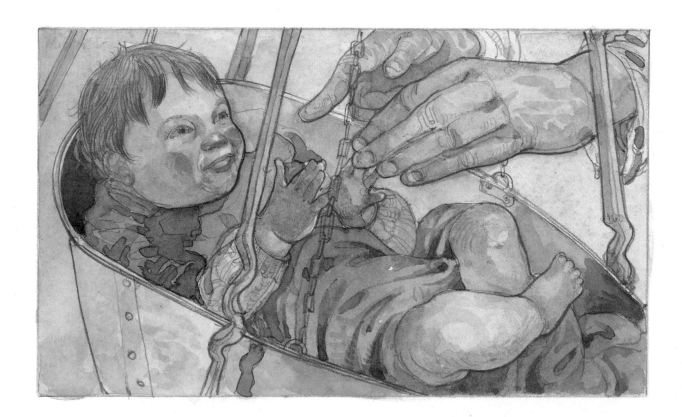

The baker, the piper, the mother, the father, and the baby went with Jack to the lake. There, under an elm tree, stood the beautiful maiden, waiting.

"Ah, there is the man with his heart in a bucket!" teased the maiden.

"Not so," said Jack. "My heart is in the right place now." He smiled at the maiden, and she blushed.

"But do you know the answer to my riddle?" she asked. "Have you found three different scales of gold?"

"I have," said Jack.

> "Weight is measured on a scale,
> The notes of music make a scale,
> And a fish has scales upon his tail.
> Balance, music, and a fish.
> Now, lovely maiden, grant my wish."

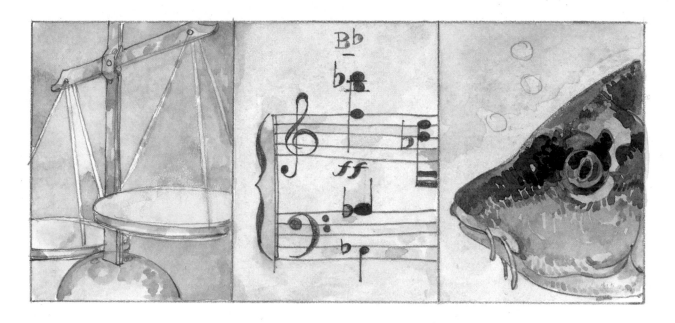

"And what is your wish?" asked the maiden.

"To win your heart," said Jack.

"You have won my heart already," said the maiden.

Jack took the small golden heart from his pocket. He and the maiden exchanged hearts. As their hands met, the two hearts merged into one.

"Take the golden heart," said the maiden, "and make two rings for you and me."

"Wedding rings," said Jack.

"Let's eat," said the baker.

"Let's make music," said the piper.

"Let's dance," said the mother and the father.

The little baby laughed and clapped his hands, and together all of them celebrated love.